Fig. 6 Bumblebee

Fig. 9 Sweet Potato Weevil

Fig. 7 Bush Katydid

Fig. 8 Slug Moth Caterpillar

Fig. 10 Woolly Caterpillar

For my dad, Byron, who
allowed me to be a sleepyhead
and whatever else I wanted to be
—E.P.

For Olaf, our entomologist
—D.S.

Text copyright © 2005 by Elizabeth Provost
Illustrations copyright © 2005 by Donald Saaf

Typeset in Klepto and Quartet.
The art was done in mixed media.
Design by Carl James Ferrero

Published by Bloomsbury Publishing, New York and London
Distributed to the trade by Holtzbrinck Publishers

Library of Congress Cataloging-in-Publication Data
Provost, Elizabeth.
Ten little sleepyheads / by Elizabeth Provost ; illustrated by Donald Saaf.—1st U.S. ed.
p. cm.
Summary: Ten sleepy insects snack, read, and play before they fall asleep, one by one.
ISBN-10: 1-58234-838-3
ISBN-13: 978-1-58234-838-4
[1. Insects—Fiction. 2. Bedtime—Fiction. 3. Counting. 4. Stories in rhyme.]
I. Saaf, Donald, ill. II. Title.
PZ8.3.P942Te 2005   [E]—dc22   2004054730

First U.S. Edition 2005
Printed in Singapore
1 3 5 7 9 10 8 6 4 2

Bloomsbury Publishing, Children's Books, U.S.A.
175 Fifth Avenue
New York, NY 10010

Ten Little Sleepyheads

by Elizabeth Provost · illustrated by Donald Saaf

BLOOMSBURY
CHILDREN'S
BOOKS

10

Ten little sleepyheads
talking to their toys.

One falls asleep
in the middle of the noise.

9

Nine little sleepyheads
reaching for a snack.

One falls asleep
on a crumbly cracker stack.

8

Eight little sleepyheads
giggling in a pile.

One falls asleep
with a dreamy little smile.

7

Seven little sleepyheads
playing peek-a-boo.

One falls asleep,
but we're never telling who.

6

Six little sleepyheads
crawling on the rug.

One falls asleep
nose-to-nose with sister bug.

5

Five little sleepyheads
begging for a book.

One falls asleep
as she tries to take a look.

4

Four little sleepyheads
toasty in their towels.

One falls asleep
while her baby brother howls.

3

Three little sleepyheads
climbing into bed.

One falls asleep when
he blinks and bows his head.

2

Two little sleepyheads
breathing soft and slow.

One falls asleep
touching shadows with his toe.

One little sleepyhead
counting back from ten.

Is he asleep?

Well, here we go again!

Fig. 1 Firefly

Fig. 4 Yellow Beetle with Black Spots

Fig. 2 Southern Green Stink Bug

Fig. 3 Red and Black Beetle

Fig. 5 Winged Desert Termite